Henry and Punkin

Printed in the U.S.A,
First Printing, 2016
ISBN 978-0-9970600-3-4

Iron Twine Press,
www.irontwinepress.com

Henry and Punkin

Lyn Coffin

Illustrated by
Reza Bigonah

4

One especially bright summer day, Henry sat with his friend Punkin on the lawn in front of his house. As you might have guessed from his name, Punkin was not a boy. He was an orangutan who slept under Henry's bed.

Punkin and Henry had been friends for a long time. Henry called him Punkin because his long hair was orange. Punkin couldn't talk—but he made really interesting noises and was smart and kind and did really neat tricks.

5

When Punkin was really pleased with himself,
he would pull a banana out from behind
Henry's ear. Then he would grin a big grin, and
balance the banana on the top of his nose.

6

After he had balanced the banana on the top of his nose for a while, he would take the banana down, peel it like a flower and eat it. Then he would throw the banana peel over his right shoulder onto Henry's lawn.

At night, Punkin folded in on himself,
so he could sleep under Henry's bed.

Henry thought Punkin was just about a perfect friend, except for one thing. Nobody could see Punkin except Henry.

Many times, Henry had tried to tell his mother about Punkin, but his mother had just smiled. "Henry," she said. "You're the only one who can see your little friend. That means he's Imaginary, not Really Real." More than anything else in the world, Henry wanted Punkin to be Really Real.

10

And Mrs. Jones, the neighbor lady next door liked to stop over when she saw Henry sitting on the lawn. She would pat his head and say "Why don't you get some friends, Henry honey?" More than anything else, Henry wished Punkin were Really Real.

On this one especially bright summer day, Henry and Punkin were looking for four-leafed clovers. They had been looking for four-leafed clovers a long time, and it was hot.

Henry was about to give up looking, and go inside for a snack. He had just about decided on having a glass of cold lemonade and a ginger snap cookie to go with it, when Punkin found a four-leafed clover, and gave it to Henry. Henry had seen four-leafed clovers before, but not like this one. This four- leafed clover was especially big, especially bright green, with especially yellow-colored flecks on its leaves.

Henry thought how wonderful it would be if Punkin were really real. Mrs. Jones and his mother and everyone would be able to see Punkin.

They would be able to see how he could take a banana out from behind Henry's ear and balance it on the end of his nose, how he could peel the banana perfectly like a flower before he ate it.

Henry's mother would laugh, though she would probably not want Punkin to drop the banana peels in the grass, the way Punkin liked to do. Henry's mother would serve two lemonades for snack, and two ginger snaps instead of one.

Mrs. Jones would stop patting Henry on the head and saying, "Don't you have any friends?"

Holding the especially big, especially bright green, yellow-flecked four-leafed clover very tightly in his left hand, Henry wished especially hard that Punkin would turn out to be really real, not just imaginary, and he threw the clover over his right shoulder. Henry was wishing so hard, he didn't notice when the big change happened.

One minute Mrs. Jones was driving slowly past the house, the next she had stopped the car outside, with two of its wheels up on the sidewalk and the driver's door open. She was running into her house without waving, yelling something that sounded like *"G o r i l l a!"*

Henry wanted to ask Mrs. Jones
if she could for sure see Punkin.
He wanted to see what Mrs.
Jones would say when Punkin
pulled a banana out from behind
Henry's ear. Maybe Punkin could
even pull a banana out from
behind Mrs. Jones's ear and
balance that on his nose.

But Mrs. Jones ran into her house and Henry heard her front door slam with a big bang. Mrs. Jones's yelling and running and slamming seemed to have made Punkin nervous, so Henry thought for a few minutes and decided it was time to go in for snack. Eating a snack always seemed to calm Punkin down, especially when he was sharing Henry's lemonade and ginger snap cookie. But this time it took some tugging for Henry to get Punkin to move.

Henry finally got Punkin to come with him into his house and they stood at the bottom of the stair. "Mom? Is it time for a snack yet?" Henry called upstairs.

Henry's mother came to the head of the stairs, and started coming down the stairs carrying a basket piled high with sheets and towels she was probably taking down to the laundry room.

"Hi, Henry," she said. "Do you want to have a snack?" Well, that's what she probably started out to say. What she actually said was something more like, "Hi, Henry. Do you AAAAGGGA AEEEFFAAHNNNOOOO,"

She dropped the laundry basket, and sort of stumbled and slid slowly behind it down the stairs.

21

"Hi, Mom," Henry said back really quickly, trying to tell her what had happened before she got the wrong idea. "I don't know if you can see Punkin or not but if you can, and I think you can, he's the orangutan I used to try to tell you about, and he didn't used to be really real, but I wished really hard and now he might be, because I'm pretty sure Mrs. Jones could see him, because she screamed 'Gorilla' and ran into her house and slammed the door."

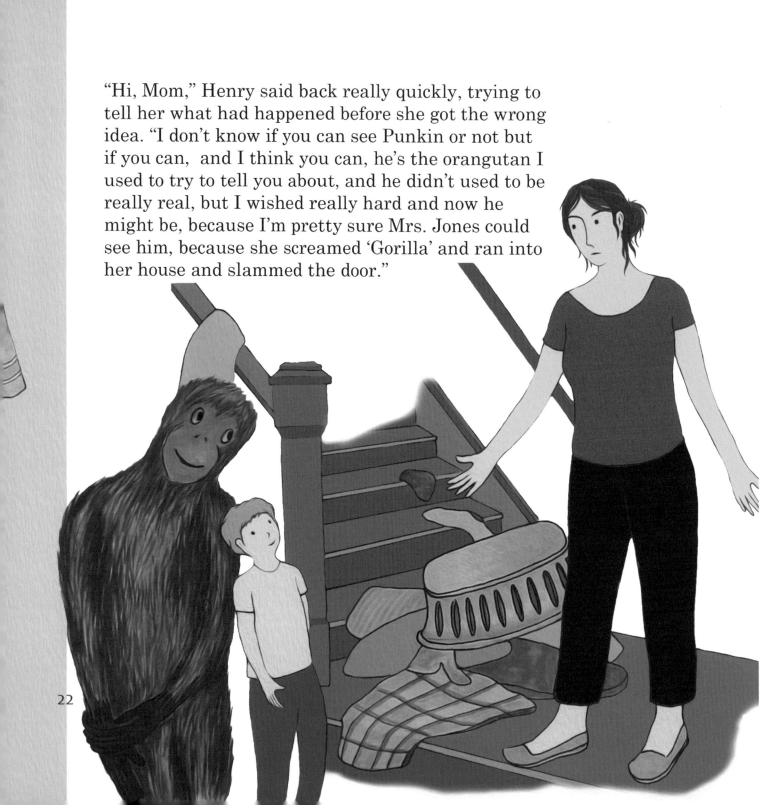

Henry said all this in kind of a big rush, which was maybe a mistake, because the strange big-eyed look on his mother's face didn't change. She had pretty much arrived at the bottom of the stairs by then, and she started coming toward Henry with her lips all pushed together the way she did when he had done something she would later tell him was "Wrong, wrong, wrong."

Behind him, Henry could hear Punkin whining and moaning, the way he did when he heard his biggest fear, which was fire engines with their sirens on.

23

"Henry," said his mother in kind of a loud whisper. "Step forward slowly." Henry did as his mother asked, and Punkin, of course, stepped forward right along with him. He was whining and moaning louder now, and Henry's mother was, too. Henry turned to Punkin, who was shaking from head to foot.

That's when Henry first heard the fire engines coming. "Don't worry," he said. "Those fire engines are probably on their way somewhere else. They're not coming here". But Henry was wrong. Before you could say, "Oh, what a mix up," there was the sound of screeching tires outside, then a banging at the door.

Henry would have gone to see who it was, but Punkin started backing away, still holding Henry's hand. Then Henry's mother reached out, and grabbed on to Henry's other hand, so for a moment, all Henry could do was stand there with his arms stretched out, Punkin pulling him one way, and his mother, the other.

When it was all over, Henry could never remember what order all the different things which happened *next*-- happened *in*.

The banging on the door stopped and the door opened. Two firemen peeked around the door into the front hall where there was Punkin, holding on to one of Henry's hands, Henry's mother, holding Henry's other hand, an overturned laundry basket and sheets and towels all over the place, and Henry in the middle of it all.

"Don't worry, son," the first fireman said. Both of the firemen came slowly in to the front hall, and that's when Henry could see one of the firemen was carrying a big net, and the other fireman was carrying a gun. "Don't shoot!" Henry said.
"Don't worry, son," the second fireman said. "It's just a tranquilizer gun."

Punkin gave a really loud whiney moan. He pulled his hand out of Henry's and started backing away into the dining room. Henry's mother pulled on Henry really hard, and since there was no Punkin on the other hand any more, pulling the other way, Henry went flying into his mother's hug.

He heard a kind of bang, which might have been the tranquilizer gun going off, but by the time he got free enough to look into the dining room, all he could see was the two firemen disappearing around the corner. Punkin was gone.

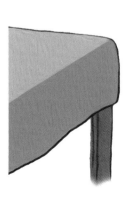

Henry's mother pulled him back into a hug. "Don't worry," Henry's mother said. "They won't hurt him if they can help it. They'll put him back in whatever zoo he came from so he can live with other gorillas."

"He's an orangutan," Henry said. "And he didn't come from a zoo!"

"Well, then they'll find a zoo and a nice place where he can live with other orangutans." Henry's mother said.

"He doesn't want to live with other orangutans," Henry said. "He wants to live here and sleep all night in the drawer under my bed."

Henry's mother smiled down at him with tears in her eyes. "All orangutans want to live with other orangutans."

"Not Punkin," Henry said. "He's imaginary."

"Everybody can see him, Henry," Henry's mother said. "When everybody can see something, that means it's not Imaginary. It's Really Real."

Well," Henry told her. "I'm sorry now I wished on the clover."

The two firemen came back into the hall. The net was still empty. "Don't worry, son," the first fireman said. "A lot of your neighbors are standing around outside, and nobody saw the gorilla come out. He must be hiding somewhere in the house."

"He's an orangutan," Henry said. "You didn't shoot him with the tranquilizer gun, did you?"

"We'll find out in a minute," the first fireman said.

"Don't worry, son," the second fireman said. "We'll find him wherever he is."

"Would you mind wiping off your boots?" Henry's mother said to the firemen. "You're tracking mud on the carpets." So the firemen wiped off their boots, and looked high and low through the whole house.

But Punkin was nowhere to be found.
"Are you sure he's not here?" Henry's
mother asked.
The firemen said they were.
"But where is he, then?" Henry's
mother wanted to know. "Where did
he go, and where did he come from?"
"There's a lot we don't know," said the
first fireman.
"We'll find out," said the second
fireman. "We'll call every zoo in the
county and get to the bottom of this."
"There's no zoo in this county,"
Henry's mother said, but the firemen
were getting ready to leave, and didn't
answer.
After that, the firemen went away,
scratching their heads and mumbling.

36

Henry's mother picked up all the sheets and towels and started picking up the laundry, mumbling about cutting down on coffee, and the high price of carpet cleaners.

Henry started looking for Punkin. He walked through the house whispering, "Punkin? It's safe to come out now." Henry looked everywhere an orangutan could be. He looked behind things—on top of things—under things. When Punkin didn't answer, Henry was really worried. He hardly ate any dinner, and went to bed hungry.

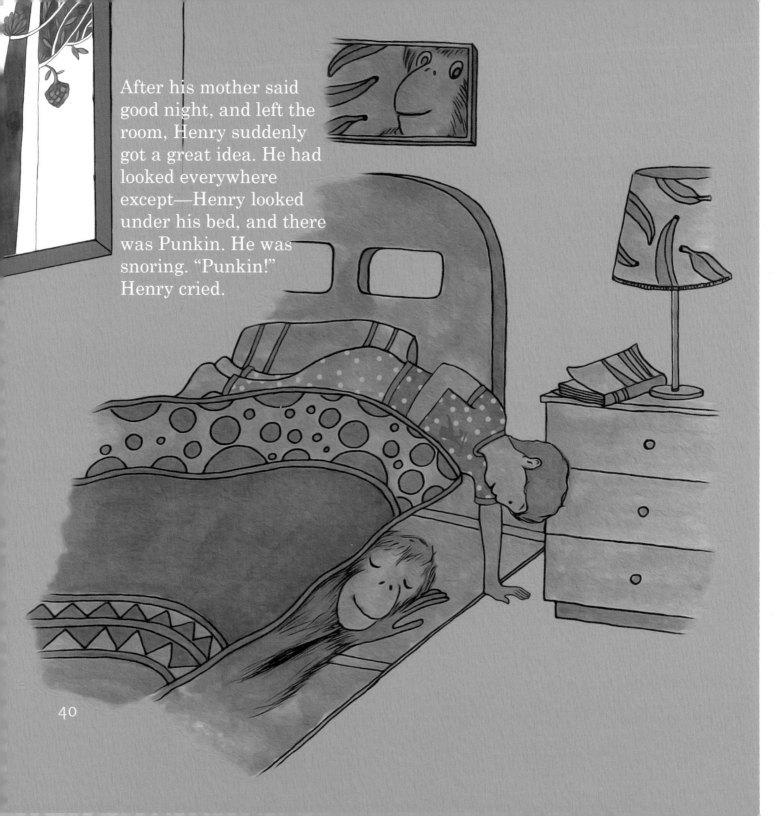

After his mother said good night, and left the room, Henry suddenly got a great idea. He had looked everywhere except—Henry looked under his bed, and there was Punkin. He was snoring. "Punkin!" Henry cried.

40

The door to Henry's room opened and the overhead light flicked on. "Henry?" Henry's mother said. "Are you okay?"

"I'm fine," Henry told her, squinting up at her. "Better than ever."

"Why were you looking under your bed? Is there something under there? Henry's mother said. She walked over to the bed, and Henry held his breath.

Henry's mother looked under the bed and shook her head. Then she stood up again.
"What did you see?" Henry asked her.
Henry's mother looked again. "There's nothing to see," she said. "Are you sure you can go to sleep after all that's happened today?"
"Positive," Henry said.

After his mother had said good night again,
and turned out the light again, and left,
Henry listened. He couldn't hear anything
now, so he reached under the bed.
"You don't have to poke me," Punkin said,
sounding a little bit grumpy.
"You were snoring before," Henry explained.
"Of course, I was snoring," Punkin said.
"They shot me with a tranquilizer dart."
"Hey," Henry said. "You can talk!"
"Of course," Punkin told him.

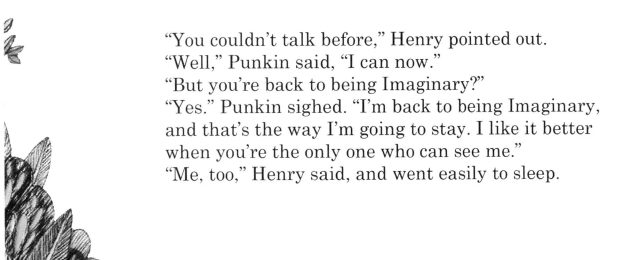

"You couldn't talk before," Henry pointed out.

"Well," Punkin said, "I can now."

"But you're back to being Imaginary?"

"Yes." Punkin sighed. "I'm back to being Imaginary, and that's the way I'm going to stay. I like it better when you're the only one who can see me."

"Me, too," Henry said, and went easily to sleep.

CPSIA information can be obtained at www.ICGtesting.com
Printed in the USA
LVIW01n2253160517
534800LV00002B/12